GREEN BAY PACKERS

BY JOSH ANDERSON

Stride
An Imprint of The Child's World®
childsworld.com

The Child's World
childsworld.com

Published by The Child's World®
800-599-READ • www.childsworld.com

Photography Credits
Cover: © Stacy Revere / Getty Images; page 1: © Africa Studio / Shutterstock; page 3: © Abbie Parr / Stringer / Getty Images; page 5: © Andy Lyons / Staff / Getty Images; page 6: © Pictorial Parade / Staff / Getty Images; page 9: © Kevin C. Cox / Staff / Getty Images; page 10: © Jonathan Daniel / Staff / Getty Images; page 11: © stevezmina1 / Getty Images; page 12: © Sam Greenwood / Staff / Getty Images; page 12: © Andy Lyons / Staff / Getty Images; page 13: © Andy Lyons / Staff / Getty Images; page 13: © Stacy Revere / Staff / Getty Images; page 14: © Patrick McDermott / Stringer / Getty Images; page 15: © Al Messerschmidt / Stringer / Getty Images; page 16: © Vernon Biever / Associated Press; page 16: © Fma12 / Wikimedia; page 17: © Fma12 / Wikimedia; page 17: © Icon Sports Media / Newscom; page 18: © NFHOF / Associated Press; page 18: © Icon SMI / Newscom; page 19: © Rick Stewart / Stringer / Getty Images; page 19: © Kevin C. Cox / Staff / Getty Images; page 20: © Christian Petersen / Staff / Getty Images; page 20: © Quinn Harris / Stringer / Getty Images; page 21: © Stacy Revere / Staff / Getty Images; page 21: © Jonathan Daniel / Staff / Getty Images; page 22: © Mark Konezny / Stringer / Getty Images; page 23: © Stacy Revere / Stringer / Getty Images; page 23: © stevezmina1 / Getty Images; page 25: © Tony Tomsic / SportsChrome / Newscom; page 26: © TSN/Icon SMI / Newscom; page 29: © J. Meric / Stringer / Getty Images

ISBN Information
9781503857636 (Reinforced Library Binding)
9781503860490 (Portable Document Format)
9781503861855 (Online Multi-user eBook)
9781503863217 (Electronic Publication)

LCCN 2021952666

Printed in the United States of America

BRINGING THE WORLD 19 68 TO YOUNG READERS

TABLE OF CONTENTS

GO PACKERS!

The Green Bay Packers compete in the National Football **League's** (NFL's) National Football Conference (NFC). They play in the NFC North **division**, along with the Chicago Bears, Detroit Lions, and Minnesota Vikings. No team in the NFL has operated continually in the same location as long as the Packers. Fans of the team have been very lucky. The Packers' 13 championships are the most of any team in all of pro football. Let's learn more about the Packers!

NFC NORTH DIVISION

Chicago Bears

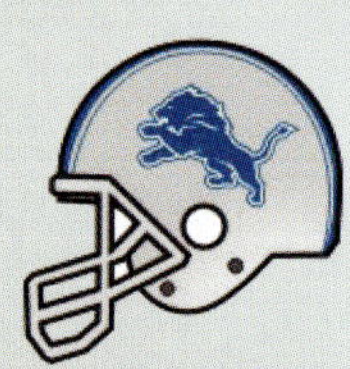

Detroit Lions

Green Bay Packers

Minnesota Vikings

THE PACKERS FINISHED WITH 13 REGULAR SEASON WINS THREE YEARS IN A ROW FROM 2019 TO 2021.

BECOMING THE PACKERS

The Packers were formed in 1919. One of the team's owners, Curly Lambeau, worked for the Indian Packing Company, a meatpacking business. Indian Packing sponsored the team by paying for their uniforms. But it insisted the team be named after the company. From then on, the team has been called the Packers. The team won three championships in a row from 1929 to 1931. Years later, under the leadership of Vince Lombardi, the Packers won the first two **Super Bowls** ever played.

UNIVERSITY OF NOTRE DAME LEGEND PAUL HORNUNG STARRED FOR THE PACKERS FOR NINE SEASONS.

BY THE NUMBERS

The Packers have won **FOUR** Super Bowls.

12
NFC North division titles for the Packers

15
wins for the Packers in 2011

560
points scored by the team in 2011—a team record!

TEAMS THAT WIN THE SUPER BOWL ARE AWARDED THE LOMBARDI TROPHY, NAMED AFTER LEGENDARY PACKERS COACH VINCE LOMBARDI.

GREEN BAY, WISCONSIN, HAS ONE OF THE LOWEST AVERAGE TEMPERATURES OF ANY NFL CITY. THE PACKERS MAY GET USED TO PLAYING IN THE COLD, BUT IT'S OFTEN HARD ON THEIR OPPONENTS.

GAME DAY

The Packers play their home games at Lambeau Field in Green Bay, Wisconsin. The building is named after Curly Lambeau, one of the team's original owners. The Packers moved into Lambeau Field in 1957. No NFL team has played in their **stadium** longer than the Packers. Lambeau Field can get so cold during the winter months that its nickname is "The Frozen Tundra." The building can hold more than 80,000 Packers fans on game days.

We're Famous!

In 2021, the television quiz show *Jeopardy* began its search for a new host. They tried out a number of different guest hosts before making a decision. One of the people chosen was Packers quarterback Aaron Rodgers. Rodgers hosted the show for two weeks. It didn't interfere with his main job, though. The hosting gig took place in the off-season.

UNIFORM

Truly Weird

With about 30 seconds remaining in a 2005 game against the Cincinnati Bengals, the Packers trailed by a **touchdown**. Packers quarterback Brett Favre dropped back to pass, and a fan who'd run onto the field came up behind Favre and grabbed the football. The fan ran more than 50 yards down the field before he was tackled by security.

Alternate Jersey

Sometimes teams wear an alternate jersey that is different from their home and away jerseys. It might be a bright color or have a unique theme. The Packers wore 1950s green throwback uniforms for a 2021 game against the Washington Commanders.

PACKERS
PACKERS PLAYERS SOMETIMES DO THE "LAMBEAU LEAP" AND JUMP INTO THE STANDS TO CELEBRATE WITH FANS AFTER A TOUCHDOWN.

TEAM SPIRIT

Going to a game at Lambeau Field can be loads of fun! Wisconsin is known for producing a lot of cheese. In the 1980s, rival Bears fans started calling Packers fans "cheeseheads." Packers fans decided to wear the insult with pride. Now many fans wear a big foam wedge of cheese on their heads when they attend games. The Packers were one of the first professional sports teams with its own cheerleading squad. But these days, the Packers borrow the cheer squads from local colleges on game days. One favorite fan tradition is grilling bratwurst outside the stadium as part of the giant tailgate party before games.

CHEESEHEAD

HEROES OF HISTORY

Forrest Gregg

Offensive Lineman | 1956; 1958–1970

Iron man lineman Forrest Gregg played in 188 straight games with the Packers under legendary coach Vince Lombardi. Gregg was selected for nine **Pro Bowls**. He anchored the offensive line for the Packers on three NFL Championship teams and two Super Bowl winners. Gregg is a member of the Pro Football **Hall of Fame**.

Don Hutson

Wide Receiver/Defensive Back/Kicker 1935–1945

Hutson was one of the league's best players in the NFL's early years. He led the league in receiving yards seven times. In addition to being the game's top receiver, he played defense and served as the team's kicker. Hutson is a member of the Pro Football Hall of Fame.

Ray Nitschke

Linebacker | 1958–1972

Nitschke helped lead the Packers to three NFL Championships and two Super Bowl victories. He was known for cat-like reflexes when defending passes and finished his career with 25 interceptions. He served as the anchor of the team's championship defense. Nitschke was inducted into the Pro Football Hall of Fame in 1978.

Bart Starr

Quarterback | 1956–1971

Starr was named **Most Valuable Player** (MVP) after the 1966 season. He led the league in completion percentage four times. Starr was the team's quarterback during three NFL Championship runs and two Super Bowl victories. He's a member of the Pro Football Hall of Fame.

The Packers defeat the Chicago Bears 25–0 to earn their first NFL Championship.

In the "Ice Bowl," the Packers defeat the Dallas Cowboys in –13 degree Fahrenheit (–25 Celsius) weather. The Packers advance to play in Super Bowl 1.

BIG DAYS

JANUARY 26, 1997

Franchise legend Brett Favre leads the Packers to a 35–21 victory over the New England Patriots in Super Bowl 31.

FEBRUARY 6, 2011

Aaron Rodgers throws three touchdown passes and Green Bay defeats the Pittsburgh Steelers 31–25 in Super Bowl 45.

MODERN-DAY MARVELS

Jaire Alexander

Cornerback | Debut: 2018

Alexander was selected by the Packers in the first round of the 2018 NFL Draft. Since then, he's developed into one of the best young defensive backs in the NFL. Alexander collected two interceptions in the 2020 NFC Championship Game. He was chosen for his first Pro Bowl after the 2020 season.

De'Vondre Campbell

Linebacker | Debut: 2021

Campbell started his career with the Atlanta Falcons and Arizona Cardinals. In 2021, he joined the Packers. He finished the season third in the NFL with 102 solo tackles. He also added two interceptions and two sacks. He played college football at the University of Minnesota.

Aaron Jones

Running Back | Debut: 2017

Jones led the NFL with 16 rushing touchdowns in 2019. He is one of only two players in league history to total more than 3,000 rushing yards and 35 rushing touchdowns while averaging more than five yards per carry over his first four seasons.

Aaron Rodgers

Quarterback | Debut: 2005

Rodgers has won the league's MVP Award four times. He led the Packers to victory in Super Bowl 45. His passer ratings during the 2011 and 2020 seasons are the first- and second-highest in the history of the NFL. Rodgers is number five in the NFL for most touchdown passes of all time.

BRETT FAVRE SPENT 16 OF HIS 20 NFL SEASONS WITH THE GREEN BAY PACKERS.

THE GOAT

GREATEST OF ALL TIME

BRETT FAVRE

From 1993 through 2007, Favre never missed a single game. During that time, he led the NFL in passing yards twice and passing touchdowns four times. Favre ranks fourth all-time in both categories. He won the MVP Award three times. Favre was chosen for the Pro Bowl 11 times and led the Packers to victory in Super Bowl 31. He's a member of the Pro Football Hall of Fame.

#1

FAN FAVORITE

Jordy Nelson–Wide Receiver

2008–2017

Packers fans will never forget Nelson's performance in the team's victory in Super Bowl 45. He totaled 140 yards receiving and gave Green Bay a first quarter lead when he caught a 29-yard touchdown pass. He led the team in receiving four times and was selected for the Pro Bowl after the 2014 season.

THE BIG GAME

JANUARY 15, 1967 – SUPER BOWL I

Four years before the American Football League (AFL) and NFL merged to form one league, they agreed that the champions of each league would play at the end of the season. The game wasn't officially called the Super Bowl until a few years later. The first AFL–NFL World Championship Game featured the Packers and the Kansas City Chiefs. Both teams were led by quarterbacks and coaches who would later be elected to the Pro Football Hall of Fame. Behind two touchdown passes from quarterback Bart Starr, the Packers earned a decisive victory 35–10.

THE FIRST SUPER BOWL WAS PLAYED AT MEMORIAL COLISEUM IN LOS ANGELES, CALIFORNIA. ABOUT 62,000 FANS ATTENDED THE GAME.

VINCE LOMBARDI LED THE PACKERS TO VICTORY IN THREE NFL CHAMPIONSHIP GAMES AND TWO SUPER BOWLS.

AMAZING FEATS

48 Touchdown Passes

In 2020 by
QUARTERBACK
Aaron Rodgers

1,883 Rushing Yards

In 2003 by
RUNNING BACK
Ahman Green

1,519 Yards

In 2014 by
WIDE RECEIVER
Jordy Nelson

10 Interceptions

In 1943 by
BACK
Irv Comp

ALL-TIME BEST

PASSING YARDS

Brett Favre
61,655

Aaron Rodgers
55,360*

Bart Starr
24,718

RUSHING YARDS

Ahman Green
8,322

Jim Taylor
8,207

John Brockington
5,024

RECEIVING YARDS

Donald Driver
10,137

James Lofton
9,656

Sterling Sharpe
8,134

SACKS**

Willie Davis
99.5

Clay Matthews
83.5

Ezra Johnson
82

SCORING

Mason Crosby
1,806*

Ryan Longwell
1,054

Don Hutson
825

INTERCEPTIONS

Bobby Dillon
52

Willie Wood
48

Herb Adderley
39

*as of 2021
**unofficial before 1982

DONALD DRIVER WAS SELECTED FOR THE PRO BOWL THREE TIMES DURING HIS 14 SEASONS IN GREEN BAY.

GLOSSARY

division (dih-VIZSH-un): a group of teams within the NFL that play each other more frequently and compete for the best record

Hall of Fame (HAHL of FAYM): a museum in Canton, Ohio, that honors the best players in NFL history

league (LEEG): an organization of sports teams that compete against each other

Most Valuable Player (MOHST VAHL-yuh-bul PLAY-uhr): a yearly award given to the top player in the NFL

Pro Bowl (PRO BOWL): the NFL's All-Star game where the best players in the league compete

sack (SAK): when a quarterback is tackled behind the line of scrimmage before he can throw the ball

stadium (STAY-dee-uhm): a building with a field and seats for fans where teams play

Super Bowl (SOO-puhr BOWL): the championship game of the NFL, played between the winners of the AFC and the NFC

touchdown (TUTCH-down): a play in which the ball is brought into the other team's end zone, resulting in six points

FIND OUT MORE

IN THE LIBRARY

Bulgar, Beth and Mark Bechtel. *My First Book of Football.* New York, NY: Time Inc. Books, 2015.

Jacobs, Greg. *The Everything Kids' Football Book, 7th Edition*. Avon, MA: Adams Media, 2021.

Sports Illustrated Kids. *The Greatest Football Teams of All Time*. New York, NY: Time Inc. Books, 2018.

Wyner, Zach. *Green Bay Packers*. New York, NY: AV2, 2020.

ON THE WEB

Visit our website for links about the Green Bay Packers:
childsworld.com/links

Note to parents, teachers, and librarians: We routinely verify our web links to make sure they are safe and active sites. Encourage your readers to check them out!

INDEX

ABOUT THE AUTHOR

Josh Anderson has published over 50 books for children and young adults. His two boys are the greatest joys in his life. Hobbies include coaching his sons in youth basketball, no-holds-barred games of Apples to Apples, and taking long family walks. His favorite NFL team is a secret he'll never share!